Water
Water

JESSICA BROMLEY BARTRAM

Published in Canada by Fitzhenry & Whiteside, 195 Allstate Parkway, Markham, ON   L3R 4T8

Published in the United States by Fitzhenry & Whiteside, 311 Washington Street, Brighton, MA 02135

2 4 6 5 3 1

Library and Archives Canada Cataloguing in Publication

Title: Water water / Jessica Bromley Bartram.
Names: Bartram, Jessica Bromley, author, illustrator.
Identifiers: Canadiana 20200339176 | ISBN 9781554555567 (hardcover)
Subjects: LCSH: Lake ecology–Juvenile literature. | LCSH: Lakes–Juvenile literature.
Classification: LCC QH541.5.L3 B37 2021 | DDC j577.63–dc23

Fitzhenry & Whiteside acknowledges with thanks the Canada Council for the Arts and the Ontario Arts Council for their support of our publishing program. We acknowledge the financial support of the Government of Canada through the Canada Book Fund (CBF) for our publishing activities.

 Canada Council   Conseil des arts
for the Arts   du Canada

ONTARIO ARTS COUNCIL
CONSEIL DES ARTS DE L'ONTARIO
an Ontario government agency
un organisme du gouvernement de l'Ontario

Publisher Cataloging-in-Publication Data (U.S.)

Names: Bartram, Jessica Bromley, author, illustrator.
Title: Water, Water / Jessica Bromley Bartram.
Description: Markham, Ontario : Fitzhenry and Whiteside, 2021. | Summary: "A young girl is spending a summer at the lake and experiencing the worlds she finds (and imagines) both under the water and above. From striped rocks under the surface to water snails, crayfish to gulls, loons and swallows flying overhead she sees all the life around the watery habitat. And who knows what creatures can be found in the deepest waters"-- Provided by publisher.
Identifiers: ISBN 978-1-55455-556-7 (hardback)
Subjects: LCSH: Lake animals – Juvenile fiction. | Lake ecology – Juvenile fiction. | BISAC: JUVENILE FICTION / General.
Classification: LCC PZ7.1B378Wat | DDC [E] – dc23a

Cover and interior design by Tanya Montini

Printed in Hong Kong by Sheck Wah Tong Printing

www.fitzhenry.ca

To my dad,
who brought us to the island,
my mom, who has kept us there,
and to Georgian Bay,
my heart's home.

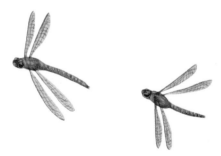

When the day is calm, I slip beneath
the surface and the lake breathes
around me, slants of sunlight shimmering
through its green-water body.

Diving down, I trace the striped
rocks that run rippling below me,
following clouds of minnows that
flash silver as they swim.

I see water snails creeping over tumbled rocks, a bass tending to its nest, and a bright blue crayfish deep in a shadowy crevice that waves a snippity claw at me as I pass.

When I come up for air, the swallows swoop above me and the lake sighs, stretching out between green islands and over the horizon, looking as endless as the sea.

In the evening, the sunset glows across the
water, the lake drinking the sun's sinking
as the gulls settle, sleepy on their shoals.

Once night tiptoes in and the stars scatter
across the sky, the call of a loon drifts through
the dark and winds its way into my dreams.

In the morning, the water is threaded with ribbons of cold, come up from the deep on a midnight wind.

Then the bass swim fast, darting from rock to rock, and the open water leans in, dancing over the shoals, hinting at storms to come.

Some shoals are animals in disguise: an elephant swimming the channel, the Loch Ness monster stretching its neck, a whole pod of whale's backs, speckled and striped, always just about to dive.

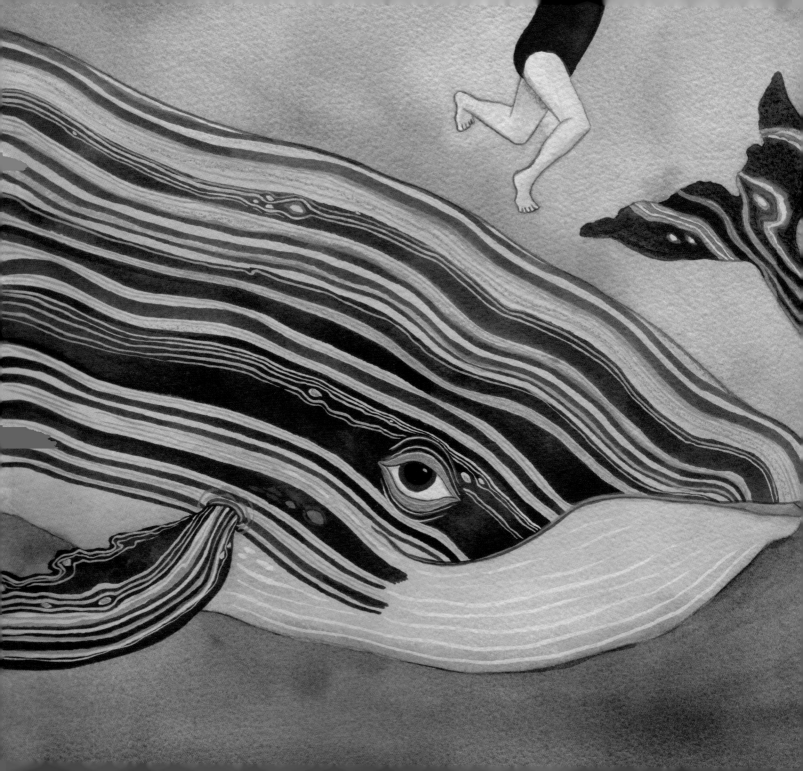

As I swim between them, I imagine the whale's backs
waking, lifting granite tails up from the lake bed as
they come to life, one wise old eye rolling my way
as I watch them disappear into the deep water,
a part of the lake I'll never know.

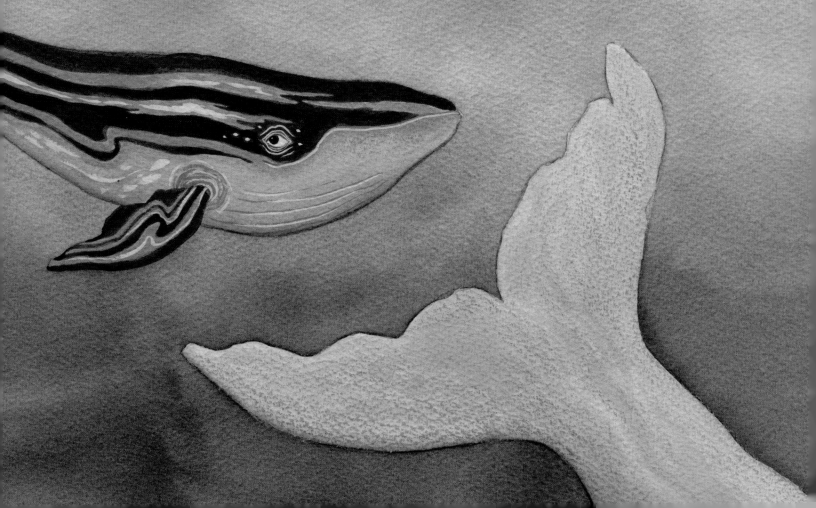

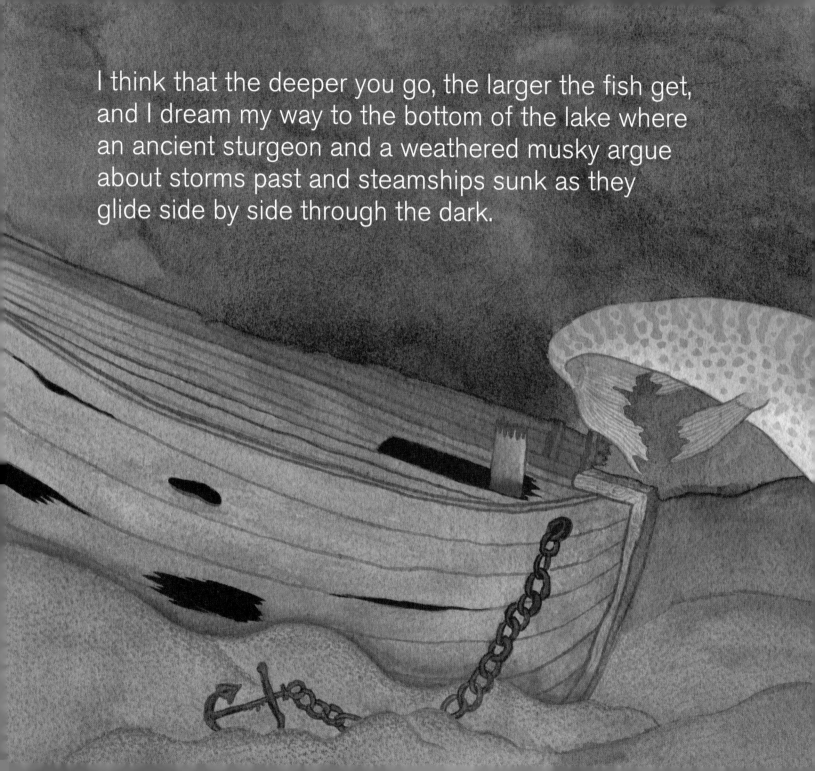

I think that the deeper you go, the larger the fish get, and I dream my way to the bottom of the lake where an ancient sturgeon and a weathered musky argue about storms past and steamships sunk as they glide side by side through the dark.

When the evening wind swoops in, swifter than a swallow, I'm sure I can hear their voices flung up onto the heads of whitecaps, whipping towards me across the gale.

Their words weave through every trough and crest until the lake is filled with stories that whisper around me into the night, telling of lighthouses and monster waves, ghost ships and black water.

In the morning, the wind is gone and the water laps softly against the shore. Dragonflies zip overhead as I step into the lake.

I float on my back as the lake curls itself around me, sleepy after the wildness of the storm.